WELCOME TO
ALIEN SCHOOL

For Steff and Frank, with love – CH
In memory of Sharon, with love xx – EE

SIMON AND SCHUSTER
First published in Great Britain in 2012
by Simon and Schuster UK Ltd
1st Floor, 222 Gray's Inn Road, London WC1X 8HB
A CBS Company

Text copyright © 2012 Caryl Hart (www.carylhart.com)
Illustrations copyright © 2012 Edward Eaves

A CIP catalogue record for this book is available from the
British Library upon request

ISBN: 978-0-85707-257-3
Printed in China
10 9 8 7 6 5 4 3 2 1

WELCOME TO
ALIEN SCHOOL

CARYL HART & ED EAVES

SIMON AND SCHUSTER
London   New York   Sydney   Toronto   New Delhi

"Red-Five? Red-Five?
This is Mission Control.
Get ready for countdown."

5 4 3

2 1 BLAST OFF!

It's great playing space explorers. I am just about to launch my new rocket when . . .

"Albie!"

Uh-oh!
Time for school!

Mum hands me my bag
and we climb into the car.

The car whooshes up into the air,
through the clouds and out into

S P A

"**Woah!** This is **awesome!**" I gasp.
We cruise past planets and comets and stars,
then swoop towards a strange spotty planet.

Mum puts the brakes on and we glide to the ground.
There are spaceships **everywhere!**
Mum opens the door and tells me to hop out.
"Have a good day," she says.

ALIEN SCHOOL

"WAIT!" I cry.
"This isn't my school!"
But it's too late.

Suddenly, an **enormous** shaggy alien appears.
"What's your name?" it growls.
"I'm Albie," I tremble. "Please don't eat me!"

"Oh, I never eat my friends!" grins the alien.
"I'm Nogel. Come on, or we'll be late."

Our teacher is called Mr Krark. He looks **very** strange indeed.

"Welcome to Alien School," he gurgles.

Everyone is staring at me. I try to blend in but Mr Krark asks the class to guess what kind of creature I am. It's **SO** embarrassing!

"Is it an Oggle-Blomp?" asks a pink alien.
"No, it's a Durkle!" says a long-nosed yellow creature.

"Actually," says Mr Krark, "Albie is a Human from Planet Earth. But don't worry, I'm sure he's very friendly and almost certainly won't bite."

First, we have to do spellings.

"Spell bazoozle-squark," says Mr Krark.
"Spell flobbedy-oobeddy-pom-pom."
"Spell tog-tog-de-noggle-plomp."

This is hopeless.
I can't spell **anything**.

"Don't worry," says Nogel.
"It's always hard at first."

Next we have to do sums. Now I **love** maths,
but space sums are impossible.
I can't even recognise the numbers!
Just then a loud alarm starts to ring.
PHEW!

"**Lunchtime!**" shouts Nogel,
and we all rush for the door.

The canteen is packed with the strangest creatures I have ever seen. Nogel pushes a button on a green nozzle and — splurrrkkk! — something lands on my plate. EWWWW!

"Mmmm, space-ghetti! My favourite," grins Nogel.
"Are you sure it's OK?" I whisper. "It seems to be glowing!"

After lunch, it's messy time. I paint a fierce T-rex but space paints must be magic because the T-rex comes to life!

Uh-oh!

Quick as a flash, Nogel shoves a painted lollipop between its teeth. That should keep it quiet.

We tidy up our things, then rush outside to play.
"Let's ride the scooters!" shouts Nogel.

Riding a scooter at home is easy, but
these ones look a bit more tricky!

Nogel zooms off. "Just push the red button and hold on tight!" he says. But there are **loads** of buttons and they are **all** red!

I don't know which one to press, so I try them all and . . .

WOOOAAAHHH!

The scooter flips and twists and I tumble through the sky!

Heeellllppp!
I'm heading for outer space!

Suddenly something grabs me around the waist.

It's Mr Krark's long arms! I'm saved!
"It looks like you could do with some
scooter lessons," he laughs.

Nogel rushes up and gives me a big hug. "Sorry, Albie," he mumbles. "I thought you had ridden one before."

"That's OK," I say. "It was **amazing**."

All too soon, it's hometime. I rush up to Mum.
"Can Nogel come for tea?" I ask.

Mum smiles at my new friend. "That would be lovely," she says, "But Albie has swimming tonight."

"See you tomorrow then," I sigh.
"Have fun at the pool!" calls Nogel.

Uh-oh!